NO MORE TELEVISION!

Story and Pictures by
Philippe Dupasquier

Ⓐ
Andersen Press • London

For Bruce - who helped build the tree house

First published in Great Britain in 1995 by Andersen Press Ltd., 20 Vauxhall Bridge Road, London SW1V 2SA.
This paperback edition first published in 1999 by Andersen Press Ltd. Published in Australia
by Random House Australia Pty., 20 Alfred Street, Milsons Point, Sydney, NSW 2061.
All rights reserved. Colour separated in Italy by Fotoriproduzioni Grafiche, Verona.
Printed and bound in Italy by Grafiche AZ, Verona.

10   9   8   7   6   5   4   3   2   1

British Library Cataloguing in Publication Data available.

ISBN 0 86264 891 2

This book has been printed on acid-free paper

Like most families, the Dixons had a television.

Everyone enjoyed watching it.

Mrs Dixon liked the comedies and the keep-fit programmes best.

Mr Dixon liked the motor racing and never missed the cookery course.

But the children never missed anything at all.
They spent hours in front of the television. They watched it after school, in the evening, after dinner and all weekend, switching from channel to channel. They couldn't get enough of it.

They never did their homework, they never played outside. And because of the television they never did anything to help.

Mr and Mrs Dixon didn't like it.

One day, Mr Dixon had enough. He unplugged the television, carried it upstairs and put it in the old wardrobe.

"From now on, you will watch it only at weekends," he said.

The children were furious.

But of course, on Tuesday, Mr Dixon had to carry it back for Mrs Dixon's keep-fit programme.

And on Wednesday he did the same for his cookery course.

On Thursday,
Kate had to watch a very important documentary for her history lesson.

And on Friday it was the second part of "The Black Stallion". Nobody could miss that!

Unfortunately for Mr Dixon, the television was very heavy. Once, he tripped and fell down the stairs and almost broke his neck as well as the television.

Eventually, he gave up carrying it and the children went back to their old habits.

Mr and Mrs Dixon despaired.

Then one day, when Mr Dixon was in town, he saw a sign in the window of the second-hand shop. It said: 'Second-hand television for sale'.

Mr Dixon had a good look in the window and smiled. He had an idea.

That afternoon, when the children came back from school, the television was gone.

"There will be no more television in this house," declared Mr Dixon. "I took it to the second-hand shop to sell it."

The children rushed upstairs, but there was no television in the wardrobe. Of course they did not believe Mr Dixon.

"Come on, Dad, where have you put it?" they kept asking.

But the next morning, on their way to school, the children saw for themselves...

There, in the window of the second-hand shop, sat their very own television. The children could not believe it. Mrs Dixon was quite surprised as well, but she quickly agreed it could not do them any harm.

The following week, Mr and Mrs Dixon worked hard to take their children's minds off the television.

Mr Dixon brought back all sorts of interesting books from the library for Tim.

Mrs Dixon bought some material and made a rabbit for Ben to complete his teddy collection.

She also helped Kate with her piano practice.

On Thursday, Mr Dixon took the boys shopping and they cooked a terrific dinner.

Later that week, Mrs Dixon found the forgotten board games at the bottom of a drawer.

On Saturday, the television in the window of the second-hand shop had gone. It had been sold.

The children were very depressed.

"Come on, cheer up, it's not the end of the world," said Mr Dixon and that day he bought some wood, ropes and tools and on Sunday they started to build a tree house in the garden.

Slowly, the days passed and the children began to forget the television. They might have forgotten it completely if one day something quite extraordinary hadn't happened.

They were having fun dressing up; they had found lots of old clothes in the attic when suddenly...they saw it! They couldn't believe their eyes—there right in front of them was the television!

"DAAAAD!" they all screamed together. It was time for an explanation.

Mr Dixon confessed everything. He had never taken the television to the shop...but when he had seen the very same television in the shop window that day, it had given him the idea of hiding their own television in the attic.

"I was going to put it back sooner or later," he said. Everyone was flabbergasted.

"You mean we could have watched 'The Black Stallion'?" exploded Mrs Dixon.

"Well, it's on tonight, if you want to catch up..." said Mr Dixon, feeling quite guilty.

"Oh, yes!! Let's have it back, Dad," shouted the children.

So Mr Dixon brought the television back downstairs and they all watched it that weekend...They also watched it the following week because Mr Dixon did not have the heart to put it back in the wardrobe.

But everything was not quite like it had been before, because that very same week...

Tim finished all his library books
and tidied his room.

Kate became a millionaire in one evening...

and Ben made a house for his teddies.

They all made a magnificent cake for Mrs Dixon's birthday.

As a special present, they organised a concert.

But best of all, they finished the tree house and invited all their friends to a party to celebrate. Everybody had a great time. Well, except Mr Dixon…

...he was watching television.

More Andersen Press paperback picture books!

THE PICNIC
by Ruth Brown

OUR PUPPY'S HOLIDAY
by Ruth Brown

FRIGHTENED FRED
by Peta Coplans

A COUNTRY FAR AWAY
by Nigel Gray and Philippe Dupasquier

THE MONSTER AND THE TEDDY BEAR
by David McKee

THE HILL AND THE ROCK
by David McKee

MR UNDERBED
by Chris Riddell

MICHAEL
by Tony Bradman and Tony Ross

FROG IN LOVE
by Max Velthuijs

THE TALE OF MUCKY MABEL
by Jeanne Willis and Margaret Chamberlain

THE TALE OF GEORGIE GRUB
by Jeanne Willis and Margaret Chamberlain